NO PLACE LIKE HOME

Written and illustrated by

RONOJOY GHOSH

Eerdmans Books for Young Readers

Grand Rapids, Michigan

George never smiled.

He never spoke to anyone.

In fact, George was quite the

grump.

George didn't even
like ice cream.

And he definitely didn't
like his house.

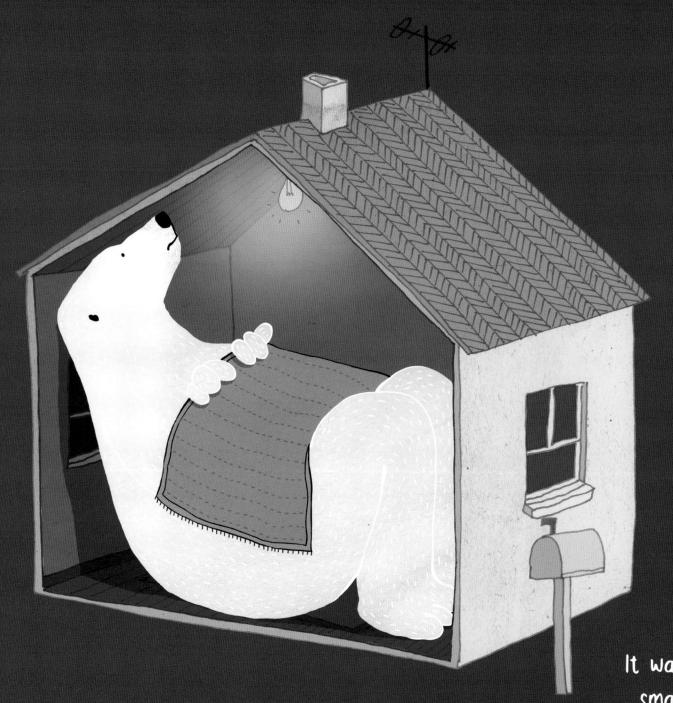

It was much too
small for him.

The city was no place
for a polar bear like George.

It was crowded, and
George didn't like crowds.

All George wanted was
to go back home.
But he had forgotten
where home was.

He knew the city
didn't feel like home.

But he didn't like
sleeping in trees.

George tried living on a mountain.

But he didn't like heights.
They scared him.

Maybe the desert was home?

No, the desert was too hot,
and it made George thirsty.

What about the sea?

The sea was better.
George liked being in the water.

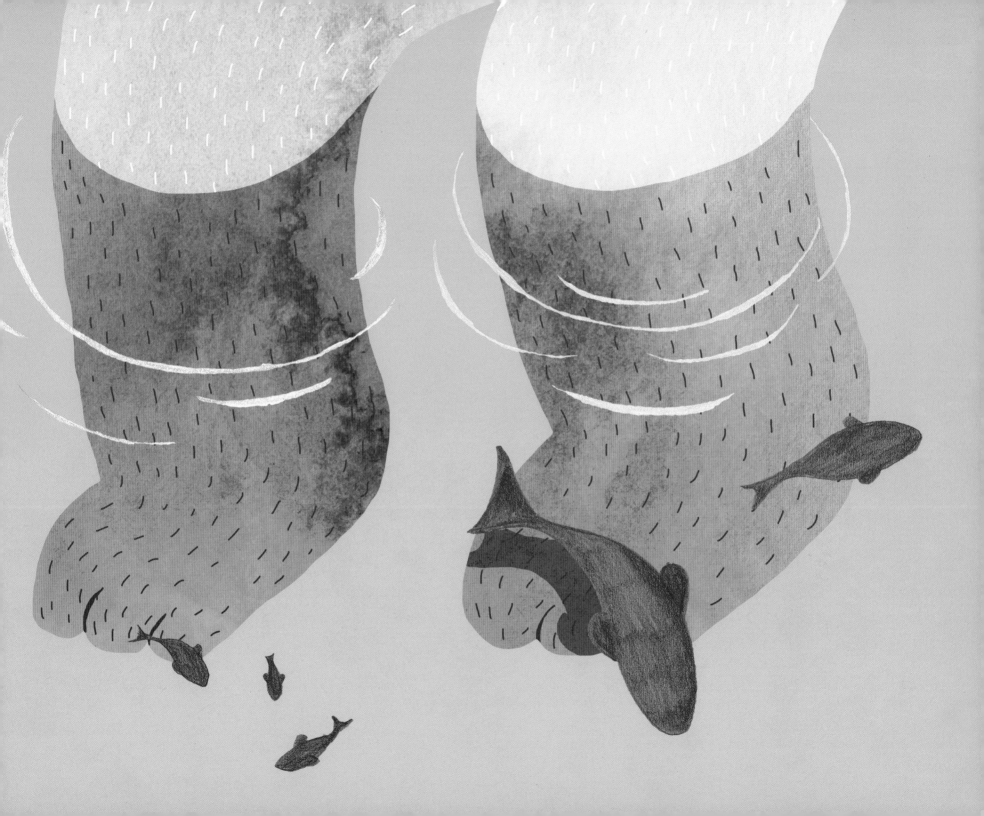

But sometimes the sea
made him nervous.

Hmmm, the sea wasn't home.

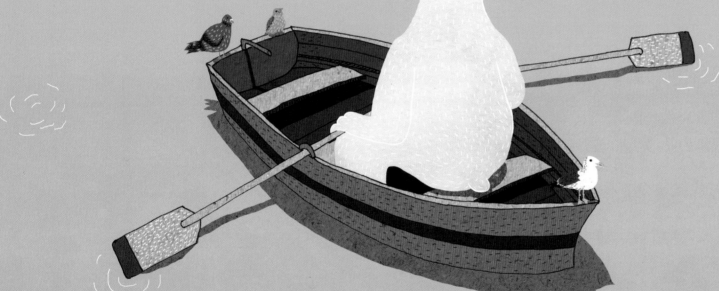

George rowed sadly for days
and days until he came to
a strange white land.

George liked this place.
It was cold and covered with ice
as far as he could see.

George wasn't grumpy anymore.
After all his travels, he was
sure of one thing.

There is no place
like home.

Ronojoy Ghosh has been an art director in the advertising industry for almost twenty years. His first children's book, *Ollie and the Wind* (Penguin Random House Australia) was shortlisted for Book of the Year by the Children's Book Council of Australia in 2016. He currently lives in Australia with his family. Visit his website at www.ronojoyghosh.com.au.

For my cloud painter.

— R.G.

First published in the United States in 2019 by
Eerdmans Books for Young Readers,
an imprint of Wm. B. Eerdmans Publishing Co.
4035 Park East Court SE, Grand Rapids, Michigan 49546
www.eerdmans.com/youngreaders

Text and illustrations © 2016 Ronojoy Ghosh
First published by Random House Australia Pty Ltd.
This edition published by arrangement with
Penguin Random House Australia Pty Ltd.

Manufactured in China

28 27 26 25 24 23 22 21 20 19   1 2 3 4 5 6 7 8 9

Library of Congress Cataloging-in-Publication Data

Names: Ghosh, Ronojoy, author, illustrator.
Title: No place like home / by Ronojoy Ghosh.
Description: Grand Rapids, MI : Eerdmans Books for Young Readers, 2019. |
    Summary: George the polar bear, unhappy living in a city, sets out to find
    where he belongs but the jungle, a mountain, the desert, and even the sea
    feel uncomfortable.
Identifiers: LCCN 2018038289 | ISBN 9780802855220 (hardback)
Subjects: | CYAC: Polar bear—Fiction. | Bears—Fiction. |
    Animals—Habitations—Fiction. | Humorous stories.
Classification: LCC PZ7.1.G496 No 2019 | DDC [E]—dc23 LC record available at
https://lccn.loc.gov/2018038289

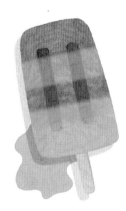

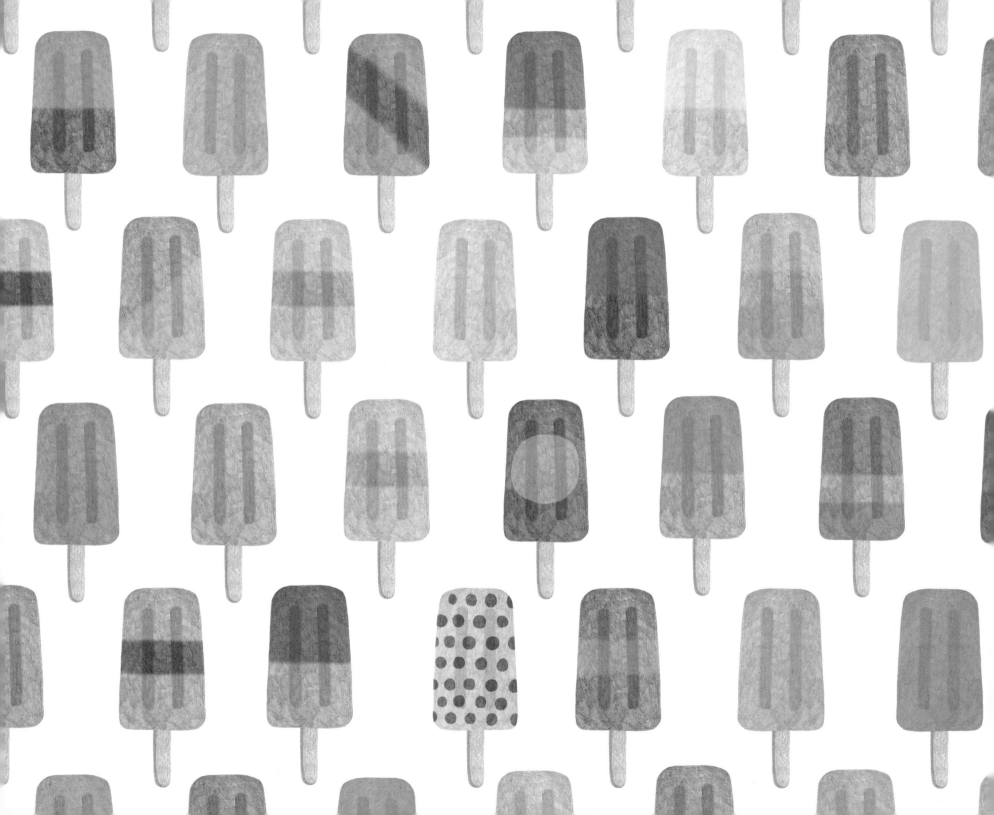